Guido van Genechten

# Because I love you so much

Splash! - Tadcaster - United Kingdom

Snowy was very smart indeed.

He knew where the yummy fish hid,
and how to catch them.

He knew how a snowflake tasted
as it melted on his tongue.

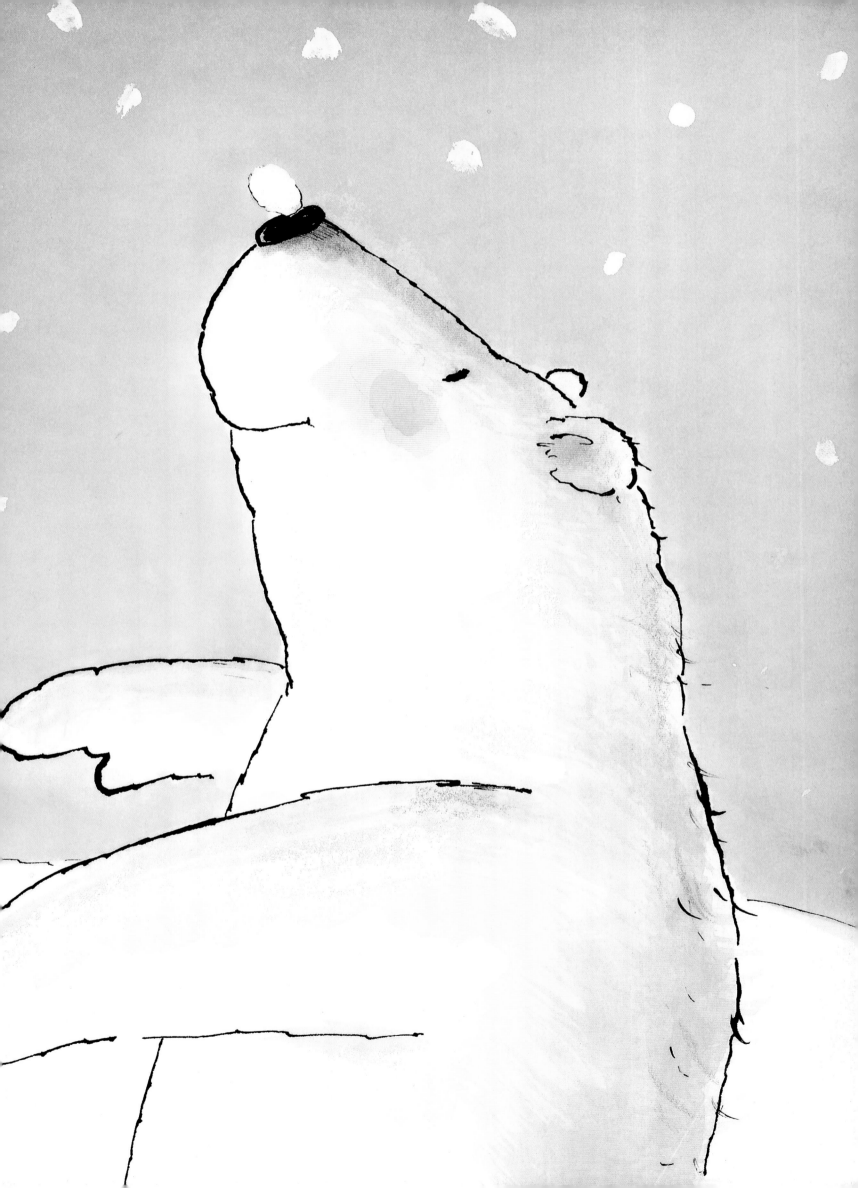

He knew that the cold, cold wind could bite sometimes.
And he knew that it could gently stroke,
or was that the touch of Mummy's nuzzling nose?

He knew how to climb an iceberg.
And he knew how to slide down it safely.

He knew that ice could crack
till it split and cut him off from Mummy.

He knew the sun came out during daytime,
then the moon shone all through the night.

All these things (and a lot more, of course), Snowy knew...

But there were a few little things - a few teeny-weeny mere trifles - he couldn't understand...

"Where does snow come from, Mummy?"

"Well, Snowy," Mummy began, "snow starts off its life as seawater.
Far, far away from here the sun shines on the sea and warms it up.
Tiny droplets of water float to the sky and gather in a cloud.
The wind blows that cloud over here.
And here the cloud shivers with cold.
When the cloud shakes, it snows!"

(Snowy now understood why a snowflake tasted so lovely: he smelled the sea in it.)

"But why is the snow white
and not blue like the sea?"

That was a difficult one.
"Hmm..." Mummy pondered,
(Mummy doesn't always know all the answers).
"Snow is always white,
like polar bears are always white."

"And why are polar bears always white?"
Snowy wanted to know.

"Because white is the sweetest, dearest and most
beautiful colour for a polar bear," Mummy said.

"And if I were bright, bright yellow," Snowy asked,
"would you still think me sweet and dear?"

"Of course," Mummy said.

"And if I were red or green
or blue all over?
Would you still...?"

"Sure I would," Mummy smiled.

"Why?" Snowy asked.

"Because I love you so

"...uch," Mummy said.

But that, Snowy already knew.